M. DI TURI
The Vassals of Bacadh

La Pereza Ediciones

Original Title: *Los avatares de Bacadh*
The Vassals of Bacadh
© Michele di Turi
© La Pereza Ediciones, Corp

© Translated by Karoline Gonzalez

First Edition in English

ISBN-9781623751654

Illustration by: © Julio Rafael Castellano Cadevilla

THE VASSALS OF BACADH

M. DI TURI

I would be incapable of dedicating these
stories to someone.
In life we pursue dreams
and nightmares haunt us.

THE MANSION OF BARLOMÉ

Through its ruined facade crawled the abundant vegetation that covered almost the entirety of the chamber, progressively taking possession of the immense mansion. Vines, ivy and all kinds of plants typical of the region became part of its infrastructure, replacing the irons that, over the years, were eaten away by rust. There are those who with certainty claimed they had seen how the autumn winds made the structure sway erratically due to its flimsy frame. Others, in total contrast, swore in the name of the perpetuity of that mansion: "I will keep silence until the Barlomé mansion falls", this being the phrase that came within the tacit patrimony inherited by the villagers.

Its huge windows remained tightly closed, while a thick layer of dust blinded everything that lay inside. Those who tried to reveal the secrets that hovered around the abandoned mansion, only managed to glimpse diffuse shadows that danced without harmony through the mentioned windows. Most ventured that it could be the effect of light on the same vegetation. It had managed to enter by force, covering with its greenery all the belongings of its former owner. However, the most morbid ones speculated about the enormous number of pests that swarmed in the ostentatious abode. The latter were not limited to mentioning them as rodents, reptiles or arachnids. On the contrary, they had the luxury of delimiting their abundance, which used to exceed the mansion's capacity to house these specimens, whose size was also usually exaggerated. Thus ending with its origin, which could not be more fanciful since Barlomé, the town at the foot of the hill, lacked fauna, and everything that surrounded the location was deprived of the presence of these irrational beings.

The Barlomé mansion was the sentinel of this small town, which was baptized with the name of its late owner. Its newly arrived inhabitants decided to recompensate him with the greatest of honors for allowing them to build on his lands, and once the town was named, they declared him as the first authority of it. That decoration was due to his vast knowledge of the moorland that, by then, resembled a paradise for those who yearned to live out of the reach of the ghosts of the past. Such a proclamation did not present any objection, so the old man happily accepted.

Sooner than later they realized that Mr. Barlomé was a man of unfortunate appearance and deplorable behavior. Year after year he raised hundreds of complaints directed at his neighbors, who bitterly regretted having ceded such power to such an abject and indifferent man. Without having any kind of consideration with the residents of the town, he took the bad habit of exposing his complaints first thing in the morning, making use of a defective megaphone installed at the gates of his property.

The old man was a fanatic of astronomy. He spent every night awake with his telescope, admiring the stars through every angle that was allowed from the spacious palace. The creaking sound of the hinges drove those who heard it crazy, reverberating and penetrating every home in the town of Barlomé. The man stubbornly refused to turn off the artifact that channeled his racket, claiming that he did not hear a thing, although it was more credible that he did not know how. Also, it was rumored that deep down he wanted his neighbors to arouse interest in the stars he admired and to accompany him on his evening. No one paid attention to his questionable strategies.

It had been more than a decade since the old man had perished inside his ominous home. The man was found with a huge fracture at the level of the skull that left a scarlet trail on the ground, descending the stairs. His "relatives" say, while trying to explain the event that his obsession ended up damaging his vision over the years. They also alleged that he had always been very absent-minded and irresponsible, leaving countless artifacts lying on the ground that he had acquired in order to improve the appreciation of those burning bodies. Therefore, the conjectures raised by the villagers were not so far from reality. The man had stumbled upon one of those trinkets the night a particular star caught his eye. Barlomé was about to go down the stairs at high speed and he did. The trail of blood denoted how the old man was still crawling on his deathbed with the intention of observing that star that took his breath away. Everything that happened was seen through one of the several windows before the mansion fell into the hands of flora and dust. The witness was not able to say a word in weeks, much less about what had happened in the huge house. By then the old man's body had decomposed enough to flood the landscape with the fetid smell of putrefaction that perennially clung to the structure. All attempts to find a new owner for the Barlomé mansion were in vain. The sad story of the death of its former owner scared off shoppers, and if it didn't, the horrible stench would take care of it as soon as the customer stepped onto the premises. The body was buried nearby with a generic epitaph on his headstone, since no one got to know him well enough to write anything honestly in his memory. The witness of the death volunteered to dig the aforementioned grave. At the time he still withheld the reasons.

Years passed, and passers-by watched the hilltop mansion, quiet, until the sun set behind the mountains and the rusty hinges began their obstinate concert. The hideous megaphone was found kicked out a few days after the decease, but this made no difference. It was as if Mr. Barlomé remained at home, moving between the rooms. The only explanation given was that the night wind was entertaining itself by traveling through this home of numerous and lonely rooms, which were only inhabited by the hundreds of telescopes of its former owner. One day, the restless villagers, with dark circles tattooed *in perpetuum* on their faces, wanted to put an end to that torment. They decided to burn down the Barlomé mansion that same night. When the sun went down, nothing and nobody would stop them in their mission, and they would finally be able to reconcile themselves with the dream world from which they had distanced themselves from. Each inhabitant seized a torch and climbed the hill with exaltation worthy of the predator that stalks its colossal prey. The ominous noise produced by the hinges grew worse as the men advanced, and when they finally found themselves at the foot of the enclosure, a blue specter appeared behind the heavy door that opened slowly. He took the form of an old man with parchment skin and a thick beard that resembled a burning celestial body hanging from his chin. His eyes as blue as the sky reflected each of the inhabitants who were there. In his pupils every man or woman could see themselves burning in blue flames. A few minutes of total silence passed. The specter returned to its mansion and the hinges continued to clatter, scratching their eardrums fiercely. One of the villagers, the same one who had witnessed the descent of the old man that fateful night, threw his torch affirming that no ghost would take another minute of sleep from him and if he wanted stay on his mansion so much, he could burn with it in hell. Immediately the palace was covered by blue flames, as if the entire structure had been built on resin. The mansion fell at the feet of the inhabitants of Barlomé who celebrated and lifted their hero down the hill. That night every man and woman in the town surrendered to the arms of Morpheus. No one cared about what they had witnessed in the ghostly mansion. No one, except for the young man who threw his torch.

Many years have passed since this event, the villagers still sleep. Their faces inspire dismal nightmares from which they will never be able to awaken. They find themselves prisoners of their own dreams, listening to the only sound that will keep them company for all eternity: the electrifying screech of the infernal hinges that can still be heard from the hill.

It was heard that the ghost of Barlomé could be found at the top of the hill, observing the night sky with the remains of his telescopes. It was also believed that he still wanders around town in search of the star that escaped him that night and the day he finds it, all the townspeople will wake up from their sordid dream, even just to find out that their bodies are nothing but pure putrefaction on a bed and will immediately perish. The true answer is unknown.

You may wonder how this story managed to escape from that cursed town, but as you already know, a young man was present in each of the events narrated. The witness in the fateful night; the voluntary gravedigger out of remorse for having remained silent; the same one who threw his torch at the ominous mansion when he saw his fears materialized and the only one who did not fall asleep after witnessing it. When he realized the situation he was in, he fled the town in search of help. However, his haggard appearance from insomnia, of which he would now be eternally a victim, made the implausible story more difficult to believe. Taking into account that almost no one knew about the existence of Barlomé.

A crude urban legend was what ended up becoming the hardship of that man who, resigned, returned to the plain after inexplicable years without sleep. He glanced around his old home and corroborated the state of his family and friends, still without awakening. He knelt in front of the remains of the mansion and before falling deeply asleep, whispered:

"Someone believed me."

Our reality was collapsing and this was only the first indication. I was not present at this event, but I did have the pleasure of meeting the young man. To my infinite misfortune, I believed him.

LEUCROTA

My life has changed a lot since my fortuitous meeting with that delusional traveler. The man looked emaciated, deprived of sleep for longer than a human can bear. It is said that madness is expressed through the eyes, this man had only one and did not need another to understand his state. He spoke of creatures and curses; anonymous founders and disappeared villages. Nothing that should be said in a first conversation with a foreigner. His name was Laurens, he never mentioned it, but it was embroidered on his tattered jacket next to a heart-like thing.

He seemed older, even older than me, and his hearing was failing. He never responded to the times I tried to call him by his name. I can almost assure you that he meant to ignore me when I did. I tried my best to get him to calm down, sleep, or take some of my provisions. The man would not stop talking.

"Listen to me, damn it!" He shouted now, at the same time that he took me by the shoulders, with a strength unbecoming of his starving body. "Go and see for yourself what I just told you. You need someone of our own ilk, one of us will be necessary to find a solution for this."

"Our ilk?" I asked, dismayed, trying to get him off me at the same time.

"You must believe in me! Only then will I be free from this curse, so it will stop haunting me." His voice changed and tears welled up. I just wanted him to calm down.

I´ll have to admit that for a moment I started to doubt, and I was afraid. That feeling was quickly communicated through my eyes.

"At last... someone believed me..."

I was able to shove him off. The man fell flat on his back and was clearly injured, but he ignored any pain. He had found a strange tranquility with himself.

It was midnight. The crown of the pines ripped the night sky, leaving behind hundreds of stars like small holes on the gloomy canvas that we call the firmament. I was carrying Laurens on my back. After his stress attack, he fell asleep soundly and I didn't want to leave him to his own devices in the woods.

I had started my journey weeks ago. I call myself Wöller, and this is a record for anyone who has the misfortune to walk in my footsteps. I know I am quite peculiar in my descriptions but doing so used to put bread on my table at the end of the day. I worked on writing tourist columns for the newspaper The Sentinel and I say it like this, in the past tense, because I doubt to return to that place. Scouting groups and hikers relied on my work before starting their expeditions. I located them tourist destinations and places to rest when exhaustion took its toll. My objective, at that moment, was to take Laurens to one of those places so that he would regain his strength and be taken care of. It was impossible for me to remember the last time I made a report with my advances to The Sentinel and I was a little anxious to return to civilization.

The destination was less than a day away, but the road seemed eternal. My head had started to ache and a strange emptiness took over my stomach. I wiped out all my supplies for a week. Nothing could calm that feeling. I felt fire inside me, my eyes burned and I exhaled vapor, but it was not because of the cold of the mountains. This was strange, enough that I began to play with the idea that I would need more attention than Laurens himself once we reached Sister Inés' chapel.

I had met the caring nun early in my journey. She claimed that there was nothing of interest amount those mountains beyond her chapel, which was in contrast to my partner's story. When I could make out the group in their morning activities, a strange murmur echoed in my ears and pressed against my temples.

"Wrong way, outsider."

It was a mocking, gasping voice, too deep to belong to a human. I turned to both sides, but not a soul made an appearance, that's when I realized that not even Laurens was still with me. I tried to convince myself that I had imagined everything, from our serendipitous meeting to their delusional story. However, there was a reality from which I could not escape. Like a cross on my back I kept feeling its weight on me.

Sister Inés received me with open arms. She wore her waxed hair finely pulled back like the day I met her. It was not the first time that I stopped to rest in those parts, although the air of superiority that was floating around always made me feel like a stranger. The nuns in the convent were watching me askance, and that got on my nerves no matter how hard I tried to ignore it. However, the not modest Inés, joked that the novices only practiced with me avoiding temptations.

I entered the chapel without crossing myself. This bothered Inés, but she never got to express it directly. My attention was always instantly seized by the stained glass and how their reflections marked the way to the altar above the seats. The chorus chants began to stun me for no apparent reason. It felt the same as hearing someone scratching on a blackboard.

"Are they out of tune?" I asked, wiping the sweat from my forehead.

Sister Inés frowned before turning pale before my eyes with a look of horror. She felt my face with the back of her hand to measure my temperature. She withdrew it so quickly that I knew instantly that something was wrong with me.

"Sit down, my child". The feeling attacked again as soon as she spoke the first word.

"Hush! Hush, for God's sake!"

The choir complied with the Chief Nun orders with a certain terror and curiosity. They observed me as if the antagonist of the fiction they lived was inside me. I began to hear footsteps outside the chapel accompanied by the icy whistle of the wind caressing the shell of my ear. That canine laugh shook my world again, and I was terrified of being the only one to hear it. Sister Inés would not stop talking, she did her best to be my ground wire, because I would cling to the sound of her voice to keep me conscious. All I wanted was for her to shut up right now. I was tormented, and laughter broke out again as soon as I accepted this fact.

"I know..." I heard behind the demonic laugh. "I also hate this feeling that humans give."

My mind began to detach from my body. I began to see myself from above, from the perspective of the beast that stalked me. I knew in that instant how tiny I was in relation to the world and the magnitude of the beast that saw me as its prey. That voice was my voice and its killing intent was mine. A last laugh broke out, breaking the stained glass. There was a clear error in my interpretation, that was not an animal like me, it was something superior, a hunter. Leucrota. I had certainty of its name without having to hear it and when it discovered that, it pounced on me before everything faded to black.

I woke up bedridden in the hidden cellar inside the chapel. A halo of almost liquid crimson light trickled down to my bed. It called me. I heard the voice of Sister Inés, praying with conviction at the altar. I felt peace for a moment, I tried to convince myself that it had all been a bad dream. I looked around and found my backpack resting to the side, with my little notebook sticking out of one of its pockets. I reached for it without getting up and flipped through a couple of pages to see how much of it had been a dream, and how much of it had been, a reality. The prayer of Sister Inés was accentuated as I advanced between the pages. I was relieved to see that the best observations from my last expedition were still there. Vanity had quickly won over reason. My hands began to tremble and I felt the weight of reality falling like an anvil on my chest. I was short of breath and with a small voice I read the last of my observations.

"His name was Laurens, he never mentioned it, but it was embroidered on his ragged jacket next to a heart-like thing.

Sister Inés stopped praying. I tried to get up and realized the weight of that traveler still remained on me. I climbed the stairs as best as I could, bathing in the only light I have seen incapable of generating shadow. I looked at the nun with her eyes lost in the threshold. Everything in the chapel had turned red and the tears on her face were like blood.

"Genesis does not talk about you," the nun said without paying attention to me, "but you come from it. Isn´t that right?

"Inés, listen to me. We have to get out of here."

The nun ignored my words, and as soon as I was in front of her, she did nothing but push me away with a force unfit for her age.

I fell to the ground, confused, my muscle memory was like a squiggle. Clumsily I tried to get up, but no matter how hard I tried, I couldn't get to my feet. It was then that I saw the stained glass windows. The members of the choir hung from the ceiling strung on them, staining them with their blood. I wanted to scream, but I didn't have the strength. That, or the terror itself, felt safer within me. Their faces in agony stared at me with empty sockets, the depth in them was the only thing that escaped the red hue that enveloped everything.

"What day were you created?" The nun continued with fascination. "Or did you create him?"

That canine laugh made an appearance, cracking reality. The hallway stretched out, and its ominous laugh came from all directions.

"I am the only thing that has been and always will be," the voice answered.

"You are not God," Inés replied, enraged at the insolence of the beast.

"No," the beast answered sharply, almost offended, "you are not ready to understand the existence of such a being. That will change. But not for you. This is the closest you will ever get to an audience with a God."

The shadow that had been hidden from the crimson light began to slip from the empty sockets of the choir members. It descended like a thick, viscous liquid pooling in the center of the chapel. The silhouette of a four-legged beast was present on the wood, its dimensions grew and twisted in a visceral way. With every step that silhouette took in our direction, it compressed the space between us. Huge hooves were nailed to the ground, the shadow began to be projected in our dimension giving a better view of Leucrota, who was exhilarated with the terror that it produced us. Its jaws were enormous and its fur was rough and blackened, with a wolf figure and the head of a hyena. It had taken over the name and appearance of an aberration that I had only heard of in stories. However, something told me that the old woman saw something much worse. Leucrota took the form closest to our understanding.

Using the seats in the chapel, I managed to get up to cut off the beast.

"I'll go with you, just leave Inés alone." I knew there would be no escape and the best thing to do was to use my privileged position to my advantage.

"Outsider, you are not in a position to negotiate. Besides, this is the only way it will end."

Leucrota lunged at Ines and tore her to pieces. I heard her bones crack, her skin rip and her faith fade. I closed my eyes tightly and waited for it to be over. I was unable to continue watching. I wanted to die in that instant. The sun burned my face and when I opened my eyes, I found myself back at the top of the hill. Further down the chapel remained intact, and I could glimpse Sister Inés among the rest of the nuns, just as I had found her that morning. I wiped away my tears and looked at the forest behind me. Inside, the shadowy creature with its canine smile awaited me.

"Come on, outsider."

THE LAST MEMORY

An immense translucent structure in the shape of a withered tree communes with the heavens. Its roots, enormous and inexorable, descend the hill on which they have been erected, shaping and delimiting the terrain of an abandoned town. They intertwine with the bodies of tributes cursed by The Barrier God's first avatar. The eternal victims of the dream that turned into a nightmare, are involved in an endeavor they never wanted to belong to. A female figure lies a few feet from me, her face hidden behind a large hood, and her curls, once golden, entwined across her chest.

"What is it supposed to be?" I asked breathlessly, as I squeezed my body tightly.

I wanted to interrupt the flow of fear through my veins at all costs. Being naive is to wrap yourself in the cloak of ignorance in the face of cold reality.

"Another one of his creations..." she answered through clenched teeth. A needle without a thread gracefully passed through her fingers. "The only one that really matters, not the old man, not the hunter, not you... not me. We are nothing but whims. This is the true end."

"I do not get it."

"We are not made to understand it. Just use it. This is the weapon that will end its existence. This is the will of Bacadh. This is our fate."

I woke up drenched in icy sweat in the middle of the forest. The first rays of the sun peeked out shyly in the distance, at the same time that the dark silhouettes of the pines around me resembled the jaws of a creature on the cracked and corrupted soil of those mountains. I picked up my notebook and, leaning on one of the logs, I decided to capture what I had witnessed in the dream world. I heard a strange, hard-to-determine growl that made my blood run cold. Again I paid attention to the jaws that had loomed at me before. These had begun to exceed the limits set by the sunlight and before I knew it, I was inside them again.

"Who is she?" I asked, pretending to have feigning uncharacteristic bravery.

"I don't know how long we've been at this, but I know you're not the worst out there."

A loud laugh shook the pines hard. A flock of birds shot out of these crashing into each other as they flew in all directions. The dark jaws on the ground finally closed on me and by the time I opened my eyes again, the day was over. I heard the crickets singing, previously non-existent, and with my left hand on my face I pressed my temples, frustrated.

"I need light!" I demanded with remarkable obstinacy.

Immediately afterwards I felt again how the rays of the sun warmed my face. It smelled of wet earth and when I took a look around I could see the bud of flowers that weren't there before. I took my pencil back and continued writing. The laughter of the creature still echoed in my head, but I did not distinguish if it was just a simple memory from which it was impossible to escape.

I walked until I got rid of the concept of time. Day and night could pass in fractions of seconds, and my only guide was in my notes. I had written fourteen notes since the last time I ate, and twenty-nine since I had the urge to sleep. That notebook had become my ground wire, the only thing that kept me away from what laid beyond losing myself, but I had no idea how much I could take it as true or as mere placebo effect. I feared for the day that this creature would realize it, although deep down, I felt that it always knew. It was just intrigued by how long it would work for me.

Little by little I found myself cleansed of everything that represented a memory to me. Scars and dents were the first to fade, while the pale mark on my ring finger and the tattoo on my forearm were the last. Sooner rather than later, I was devoid of almost all foreign memories of what I had experienced in the mountains. When I realized it was in vain, I stopped writing and would take no more than twenty steps before losing interest in continuing on this journey.

"Why are you stopping?" He asked with some satisfaction in his tone of voice.

The yellowish light of the moon embraced me, delineating my entire body in darkness.

The wisp clinging to the vegetation took on a crimson hue before rushing down and later condensing in front of my eyes. The hideous chimera took shape from that reddish cluster, which served as a mane for the canine skull that emerged from it. Inside their empty sockets, a shaft of incandescent light like that of the stars was escaping. Its four antelope legs were firmly positioned on the damp ground and its rough fur twitched, magnifying its nightmarish figure.

"I'm not afraid of you anymore," I replied, without looking away. "Take what you need and get this over with."

"You are lying," it said. Its words were wrapped in an ominous hiss.

Anger ran through my veins more than any fear ever felt. I stared at it with bloodshot eyes, eager to rip that canine smile out of its face. Running away was never an option, sooner or later it would find myself; it swore over and over that it would be like that between his laughter. The desire for him to kill me was more true to my thoughts than my hopes of defeating him, confirmed by the young woman who made an appearance at that moment.

"You are lying," an angelic voice dropped from behind me.

A girl dressed in a silk dress the same color as the moon was sitting on a felled oak. Between her fingers, a needle paced gracefully. Her eyes were gray, expressionless, with tiny pupils and a gaze difficult to hold. Beneath there were the same two bags of meat that were positioned just in the ray of the shadow casted by her bushy eyebrows. She approached me without disturbing a single strand of her golden hair. The moonlight enveloped her in a mystical halo, and as she walked she felt so light that it was almost as if she were floating. *Someone who, like me, did not feel tied to this world*, I thought. That was before I remembered the human weight that I still couldn't get rid of, the one that I still felt behind my back.

"Can you see it?" I asked, stunned. I had given up all hope of ever interacting with a human again, even less one capable of understanding me. "Leucrota?"

"That's not its name" She replied, frowning a little. "And if you did not fear it, you would see it as it really is."

When she was close enough, I could glimpse in her eyes the reflection of what looked like a huge ingrown nail in the shape of a scythe circling my neck. In the surrounding trees, thick curled appendages could be distinguished, breaking their bark. However, nothing compared to the terror that caused me to see that where that beast was, now an impenetrable pupil was positioned, leaving to the imagination what really was there.

"Leucrota is your last memory. You perceiving it that way is what prevents it from taking you where it wants." The girl clarified, offering me a condescending smile.

I looked back at the creature. It still did not resemble in the least what I witnessed through those eyes. Its damn smile kept harassing me and in its empty sockets the light within them shone brighter.

"And why can you see it?" I asked as if I was able to understand what she had to say, willing to believe every word in order to hold on to some logic that would make sense of the situation.

"Because it was the first thing I saw when I was born."

The night vanished under that suffering smile and with it, Leucrota did the same. For a moment I felt free, it was all over, its ominous presence had evaporated along with the wisp and at least for that instant, I felt peace again. All the evils that the hunter's company had deprived me of suddenly returned. I was hungry again, and the lack of sleep brought with it a huge headache.

"I'll take you to father," the girl whispered, more to herself than to me.

We made our way through a maze of trees, following what she called *The logging route.* The girl didn't stop talking. She was telling me how her father, the woodcutter, had cut them down to mark out the familiar ground. In the same way, she let me know without much concern how her mother had gotten lost after disobeying him. Each log that made up the logging route was marked by two diagonal cuts, and a third half-cut at the intersection. In the angle formed by where the third cut did not finish, there was a red arrow pointing in the direction of the cabin. Without ornaments or comforts. That home did its job of being a roof for rainy days and a bit more, that was enough. The last log felled on the road was laid out at the entrance and on it two initials were written, at a glance: "L" and "Z". A third initial had been cut in half by the ax that still stood on it.

Everything in the house belonged to the same set. Living room, kitchen and bedrooms, all within the same four walls. The wood creaked when you looked where you shouldn't have, and the smell of pine filled the entire cabin. I ferociously devoured bowls of meat and vegetable based broth that my tongue didn't have time to determine. Little Zoe revealed her name to me while she knitted on the corner of her bed, and inquired about mine, but received no answer. She offered me to rest on her father's bed while we awaited his return. I did not hesitate one second. I closed my eyes with no intention of falling asleep. The figure of the hunter or his true form, could not get out of my head.

"You can sleep here," said the girl, looking out the window. "The time has not yet come."

I would like to say that I paid more attention to that "the time has not yet come." But truth be told, I was exhausted before my brain was able to process what I heard. I didn't dream, I'm not really sure if I got to sleep. I was plunged into impenetrable darkness and only then did I feel… safe. I didn't want to wake up, I wanted to stay there forever. I was tired of pretending that I could continue this trifling existence. The overwhelming bliss of the ignorant was never meant for us, was it, grandfather?

"Have you been escaping since then?" It was Zoe who was speaking to me. I felt her hands on mine, but when I opened my eyes I knew that I was no longer there in the cabin, neither she nor me.

I woke up in a room that was extremely familiar to me. Model planes hung from the blades of a spinning fan; the walls were lined with maps and The Sentinel's articles. However, nothing caught my attention more than hearing my grandparents arguing in the adjoining hall again. I was in that old apartment I grew up in. I immediately pushed aside the covers draped over me. Even its texture aroused feelings of familiarity in me. As I did so, I discovered that not only had I returned to the one place that I used to call home, but was once again in the body of a child. There was only one strange exception, an incandescent light coming from a hidden volume between my pillows, from which emerged the cry of an infant.

"Grandfather! It's outside!" I instantly recognized my voice from when I was a child; I was terrified and had every reason to be.

"It's Leucrota!"

"It's all your fault," my grandmother exclaimed exasperated behind my bedroom door. "You bring him those things from your travels without knowing if they will give him nightmares."

"Okay, I'll take care of it," my grandfather answered with that foreign accent that characterized him. His carefree and unperturbed attitude brought peace to everyone just by listening to him. Everyone except my grandmother.

The poor lady gave a resigned snort, accompanying the sound of the doorknob being turned. The door slid open letting in a yellowish light from a worn-out lightbulb. The shadow of my grandfather crossed the room, but there was no trace of him, my mind had almost completely eliminated him from my memories. There was nothing left but his voice and his shadow.

"Hand it over," he said, extending his arm.

I knew in that instant that he was referring to that incandescent time that I had found. I took it in my hands and on the cover was the creature that had been tormenting me so much.

"I will not repeat it, Wöller," the memory usurper impersonating my grandfather assured me.

I looked around the room slowly and could catch a glimpse of that girl I had been seeing in my dreams. In her hands she held my notebook and in her eyes the inherent guilt of the accomplices. The memory stopped in its tracks and I called out to her with a slight gesture. She came out of the shadows calmly and moved to my bed like the girl I had found in that forest. She felt so light when she walked that it seemed to me that she was levitating. We made an exchange between the incandescent book and my notebook. She had achieved her goal, but something was not quite right. After admiring the little notebook with a certain nostalgia, I wanted to rescue that young woman absorbed in her thoughts, and it was then that I broke the silence.

"Is this what is left?" I asked, waving that set of notes that had been handed to me. When I said those words, I felt a lump in my throat and a stake in my heart, asking like one who does not want to know the answer. The young woman was silent. And I continued: "Wöller is a pseudonym. My grandfather would never have called me that or, rather, he never had the opportunity to do so. It never crossed my mind how important it would be to write my real name in this damn notebook."

"And why did you write about this moment?" She asked without malice and genuinely interested.

"Because without him I wouldn't be here, and if I had acted better I wouldn't have been through this."

My grandfather was ill, he suffered from those diseases that you hide from the kids. That night he was in my room, he suffered the last of the attacks. There was time to get him to the hospital but not enough time to save him, although I would not find out about it until later. Fearful of the inevitable consequences of that disease, I refused to confront the grief that losing my grandfather would bring. Before hearing the dire results of a futile operation, I decided to do what I would do for the rest of my life: run away.

I spent two nights wandering aimlessly through the streets of the city until I was found almost dying under a bridge by the then director of The Sentinel. I was admitted to the same hospital where my grandfather had died and, seeing no one in my room other than the young woman who had found me, I knew that my grandfather had not left alone. It would not be more than two years before I tried again to escape from reality, but from here on, the memories became blurred, thus warning of my success in that endeavor. I went back to those memories in my adulthood, when problems again whispered to me the tempting alternative of escape and deep down I knew what I had to do. I met The Sentinel director again, who was able to recognize me before I had a chance to do so. I took the position that used to belong to my grandfather, to travel the world and feel unreachable by the problems of the past, while the old woman, now the owner of the newspaper, consented to my desire to maintain my anonymity giving me that pseudonym well known.

"Why are you helping him in all this?" I asked, again not waiting for an answer that I was able to understand.

"It is our purpose," She replied expressionless, far from any hint of humanity. "Our existence is nothing more than this moment waiting to happen. Bacadh is nothing more than the barrier that exists between our reality and that of the superiors. By understanding this barrier it will disappear and he along with it. Only then will each being understand their role in this game, just like you and me."

Zoe took my hand gently and we went back to the cabin. A man bathed in sweat stood in the doorway with a gaze of horror. I recognized him instantly. He desperately searched everywhere without noticing our presence, while tears flowed relentlessly from his lonely eye. The young woman did not stop guiding me to the exit, while she watched him with the only feeling that I felt real within her: sadness.

"I am sorry, father," she said, seeing him find, tucked over a chair, a jacket with his name embroidered beside a heart-like shape.

When we came out we found ourselves facing that abysmal withered tree of my nightmares, where the concept of time and space became impractical. The origin of Bacadh in our world and the end of it in its own. It was not necessary to listen to her to know where I was, a voice within me announced: *Welcome to Barlomé*.

We climbed the hill at the same time that we observed the remnants of Laurens through the ages. I watched his first departure from the cursed town; when he returned with his wife and daughter holding hands; when in his self-denial he tried to face fate by cutting off the roots that captured his people, thus giving rise to the logging route without success and how finally, after the disappearance of his daughter, he took his place as the pawn he was meant to be

"No matter how hard he tried, he always came back to this place…" I thought aloud.

"That constant failure made him go crazy."

Losing me was the only thing capable of giving him back the utility that he had lost for the great plan being carried out.

Once we reached the trunk that stood on the rubble of the Barlomé mansion, we found his corpse on its knees with the same appearance as it had in our first meeting. Zoe kissed its forehead and made it disappear into a curtain of dust that quickly adhered to the gigantic tree. After much thought I proceeded to do the same with my notebook. Leucrota emerged from this and did the same by docking itself to the oak. The topmost branches began to embed themselves in the sky, cracking it, a celestial light covered its structure and an agonizing shriek filled the panorama. Zoe brought her hand to the trunk and wrapped in a divine halo she addressed me for the last time.

"Let's stop running away."

INDEX

www.ingramcontent.com/pod-product-compliance
Lightning Source LLC
Chambersburg PA
CBHW020812130626
46554CB00006B/2392